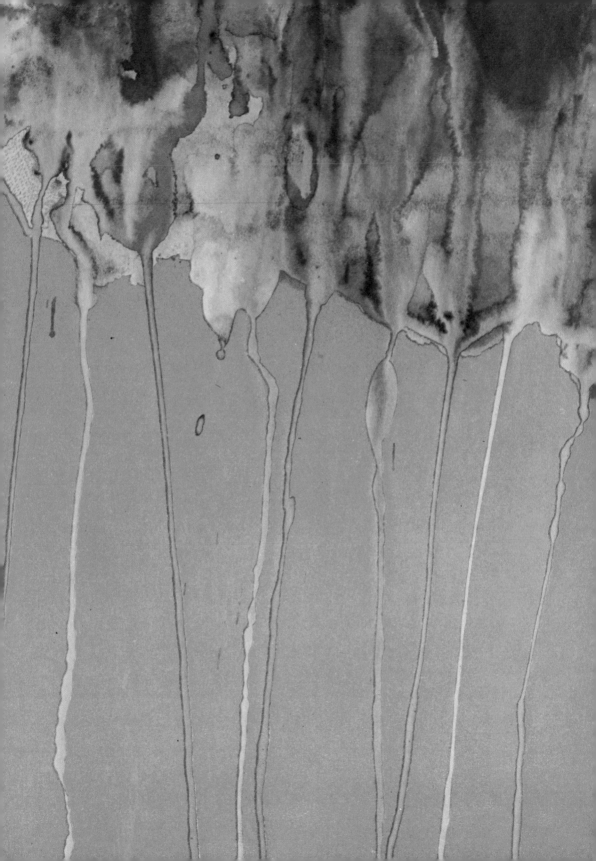

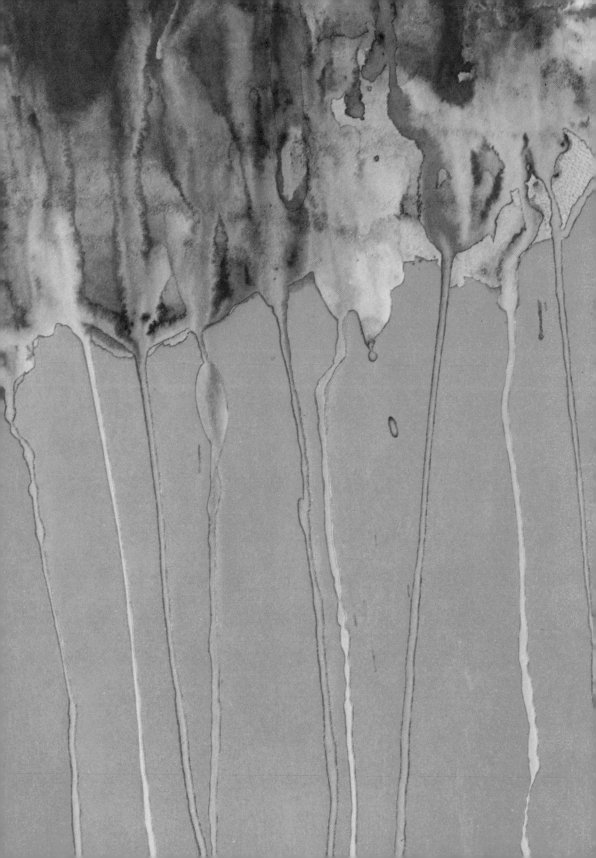

SOUND OF SUNSHINE, SOUND OF RAIN

SOUND OF SUNSHINE

SOUND OF RAIN

written by Florence Parry Heide

pictures by Kenneth Longtemps

Parents' Magazine Press — New York

Text Copyright © 1970 by Florence Parry Heide. Illustrations Copyright © by Kenneth Longtemps. All rights reserved. Printed in the United States of America. ISBN: Trade 0-8193-0422-0, Library 0-8193-0423-9. Library of Congress Catalog Card Number: 77-117555.

To my nephew, Peter Heide and to my son, Parry Heide,
for the special vision each has given the other

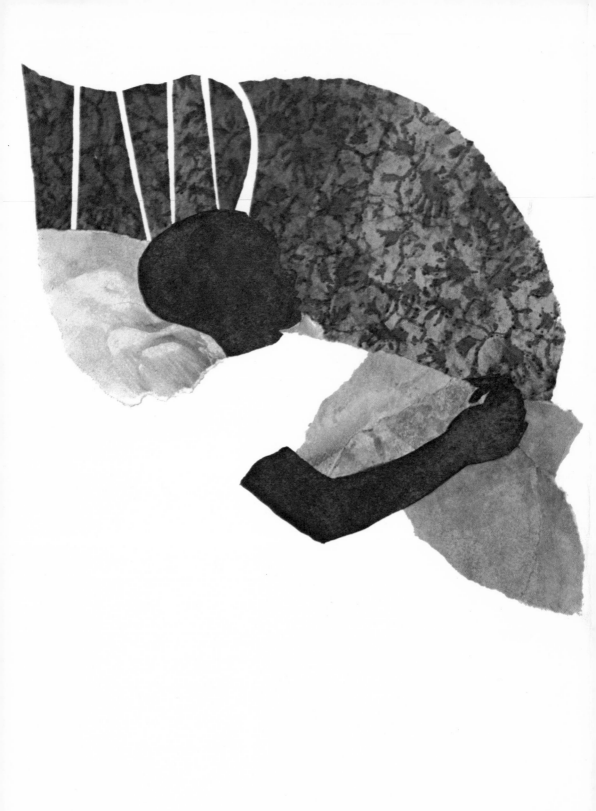

IT MUST BE MORNING, for I hear the morning voices.

I have been dreaming of a sound that whispers *Follow me, Follow me,* but not in words. I follow the sound up and up until I feel I am floating in the air.

Now I am awake, and I listen to the voices.

My mother's voice is warm and soft as a pillow.

My sister's voice is little and sharp and high, like needles flying in the air.

I do not listen to the words but to the sound. Low, high, low, high, soft, hard, soft, hard, and then the sounds coming together at the same time and making a new sound. And with it all, the sharp sounds of my sister's heels putting holes in what I hear.

Then I hear the slamming of kitchen drawers and the banging of pans and there is no more talking.

My bed is in the living room. I reach out to feel whether my mother has laid my clothes on the chair beside my bed. They are there, and I feel the smoothness and the roughness of them.

I reach under the chair to find which shoes my mother has put there. They are my outside shoes, not my slippers, so today must be a warm day. Maybe I can go to the park. I tap my good luck song on the wall beside my bed.

I put my feet on the floor and feel the cool wood and curl my toes against it.

Then it is four steps to the table, then around the table, touching the chairs, and then seven steps to the window. I put my cheek against the window, and I can feel the warm sun. Now I am sure I can go to the park, if my sister has time to take me on her way to study.

I take my clothes into the bathroom, and I wash and dress there. Hot water, cold water, soapy water, plain water, loud water, still water. Then I make sure I have turned the faucets tight. I make sure I have buttoned all of my buttons the right way, or my sister will be cross, and maybe not have time to take me to the park.

I tap my good luck song against the door before I open it.

When I open the door, I hear the voices again. My sister's voice is like scissors cutting away at my mother's voice.

I sit at the table, and my mother gives me my breakfast. I breathe on the hot chocolate so I can feel it on my face coming back warm. I drink just a little at a time so I can keep holding the warm cup.

"Eat while it's hot," says my sister to me, loud.

"Does he have to be so slow?" says my sister to my mother in her quiet voice. My sister thinks because I cannot see that maybe I cannot hear very well, and she talks loud to me, and soft when she does not want me to hear, but I hear.

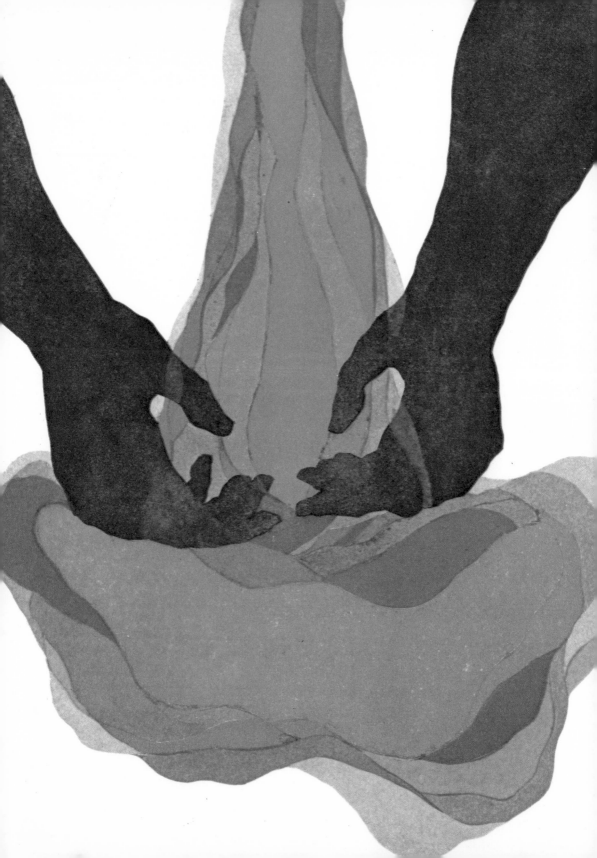

"You spilled," says my sister, loud.

"I can't be late," she says in her quiet voice to my mother. "Everybody's always late but me, and I won't be late."

After breakfast I go over to the window again, and when I put my cheek against the glass it is warmer than before, so today will be a good day. I tap my good luck song against the window.

My sister says she will take me to the park on her way to study. She gives me my jacket and tells me to wait for her outside on the steps.

I go down the outside steps. There are seven steps. Seven is my most magic number. Seven up, seven down, seven up, seven down. I go up and down, waiting for my sister.

My sister comes out. She takes my hand. She walks very fast, but I can still count the steps to the park, and I can still remember the turns. Someday I can go there by myself. I listen to the street noises and try to sort them out.

My sister's hand is not soft. I can feel her nails, little and sharp, like her voice, and I listen to her heels making holes in all the other sounds.

The park seems a long way off.

When we get to the park we go first to the bench. She waits to make sure I remember my way in the park. Fourteen steps to the bubbler. Around the bubbler, twenty steps to the curb.

I go back to the bench. I try to hurry so my sister won't have to wait long and be cross. Now seventeen steps to the phone booth, four benches on the way and I touch them all. Then I come back to the bench. My sister puts money in my pocket so I can telephone.

She talks to me and to herself.

"Filthy park," she says, and it is as if she were stepping on the words. "No grass. Trees in cages. Since when do benches and old newspapers make a park?" She pulls my jacket to straighten it.

Now she is gone and I have my morning in the sun.

I try each bench, but mine is still the best one.

I go to the bubbler and press my mouth against the water and feel it on my tongue, soft and warm. I put my finger on the place where the water comes out and walk around and around the bubbler and then I try to find my bench. It is one of my games. I have many games.

I walk over to the telephone booth, touching the four benches on the way. I stand inside the booth. I feel to see whether there is any money in the telephone, but there is none. My sister says I should always check the telephone for money, but I have never found any.

I practice dialing our number so I will be sure I have it right. Then I put my dime in and call. I let it ring two times and then I hang up and get my dime back. My sister says, that way my mother will know I am all right.

I blow on the glass and it blows back to me. I tap my good luck song on it and go back to my bench.

I play one of my games. I listen to every sound and think if that sound would be able to do something to me, what it would do. Some sounds would scratch me, some would pinch me, some would push me. Some would carry me, some would crush me, and some would rock me.

I am sitting on my bench tapping my good luck song with my shoes when I hear the bells of an ice cream truck. I feel the money in my pocket. I have the dime and I also have a bigger one. I know I have enough for an ice cream bar.

I walk out to the curb, touching the cages around the trees. I wait until the bells sound near, and I wave.

He stops. He is near enough for me to touch his cart. I hold out my money.

Now I feel him seeing me, but he does not take my money.

"Here," I say, but he does not take the money from me.

"Guess what?" he says, and his voice is soft and kind as fur. "Every tenth kid wins a free ice cream bar, and you're the lucky one today."

I can feel him getting off his cart and going around to open the place where he keeps his ice cream bars. I can feel him putting one near my hand and I take it.

I start back to my bench.

"You gonna be okay by yourself now?" the ice cream man calls, so I know he is seeing me.

I sit on the bench. I listen for the sound of his cart starting up, and his bells ringing, but I can only hear the other sounds, the regular ones.

Then I hear him walking over to my bench.

I am sorry, because I only want to feel the ice cream and see how long I can make it last. I do not want anyone to sit with me, but he is sitting with me now. I am afraid I will spill and he will see me.

He starts to talk, and his voice is soft as a sweater.

His name is Abram. He tells me about the park.

My sister says the trees are in cages because if they weren't in cages they wouldn't stay in such a terrible park, they'd just get up and go somewhere pretty.

Abram says the trees are in cages to keep them safe so they can grow up to be big and tall. "Like sides on a crib for a baby, keeping him from falling and hurting himself," says Abram.

My sister says the park is ugly and dirty.

Abram says there are a few little bits of paper, and a couple of cans and some bottles, but he says he can squint up his eyes and all those things lying around shine like flowers. Abram says you see what you want to see.

My sister says the park is just for poor folks, and that no one would ever come here if they had a chance to go anywhere else.

Abram says the park is just for lucky people, like him and me. He says the people who come to this park can see things inside themselves, instead of just what their eyes tell them.

After a while Abram goes away. He says he will come back and look for me tomorrow. I hear his ice cream bells go farther and farther away until I do not hear them anymore.

While I am waiting for my sister to come for me, I fall asleep on the bench.

I have a good dream. I dream that Abram lifts me so I can touch the leaves of a tree. All of the leaves are songs, and they fall around me and cover me. I am warm and soft under the songs.

My sister shakes me awake. "You'll catch cold lying here," she says.

The next day while I am sitting on my bench, I hear the ice cream bells and I walk out to the curb, touching the cages of the trees as I go. Abram gives me an ice cream bar and we walk together back to the bench. I do not have to touch the cages because I am with him.

After I finish my ice cream bar, Abram gives me some paper clips so I can feel them in my pocket. He shows me how I can twist them to make little shapes.

After he leaves, I feel them. There are seven paper clips.

That night I dream that someone is gathering in a big net everything in the world that makes a sound, and I am tumbled in the net with dogs and cars and whistles and busses. I try to get out of the net and my sister shakes me awake.

"Stop thrashing around," she says. "You're all tangled up in the blanket."

The next day Abram brings me a balloon.

I can feel it round and tight. It tugs at the string.

Abram says some balloons are filled with something special that makes them want to fly away, up to the sun, and this balloon is filled with that something special.

He says some people are filled with something special that makes them pull and tug, too, trying to get up and away from where they are.

His voice is like a kitten curled on my shoulder.

He tells me my balloon is red, and then he tells me about colors.

He says colors are just like sounds. Some colors are loud, and some colors are soft, and some are big and some are little, and some are sharp and some are tender, just like sounds, just like music.

What is the best color, I wonder?

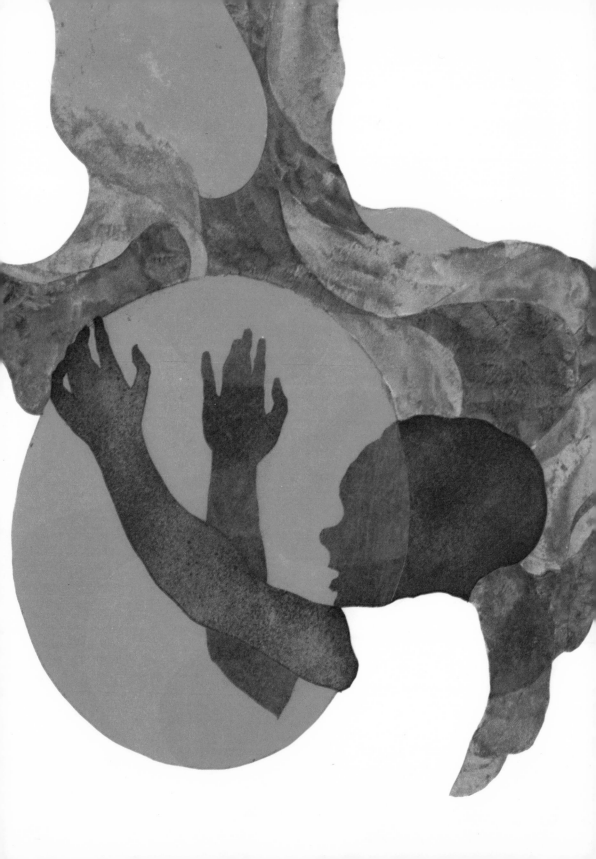

He says all colors are the same, as far as that goes.

There isn't a best color, says Abram. There isn't a good color or a bad color.

Colors are just on the outside. They aren't important at all. They're just covers for things, like a blanket.

Color don't mean a thing, says Abram.

When my sister comes, she asks me where I got my balloon.

I tell her about my friend.

I hold on to the string of my balloon while we walk.

We stop at a store. When we go in, I hold my balloon against me so it won't get hurt.

The store feels crowded. I hear a lady's voice. It sounds as if she was squeezing it out of her like the last bit of toothpaste in a tube.

The lady's voice says, "Better wait on this here colored lady first, so she can keep on going out of here and back where she belongs."

My sister takes my hand and pulls me away. I hold my balloon tight.

"So we're colored," says my sister to me as she pulls me along. "So what else is new? I've heard it a million times. I guess I heard it before I was even born."

"Abram says color don't mean a thing," I say.

My sister drags me along. I can tell by her hand that she's mad.

"What does he know? Is he black, your friend?" she asks.

"I don't know," I say.

"You don't even know if your friend is black or not," says my sister. "I wish everyone in the whole world was blind!" she cries.

When we get home, I tie the string of my balloon to my chair.

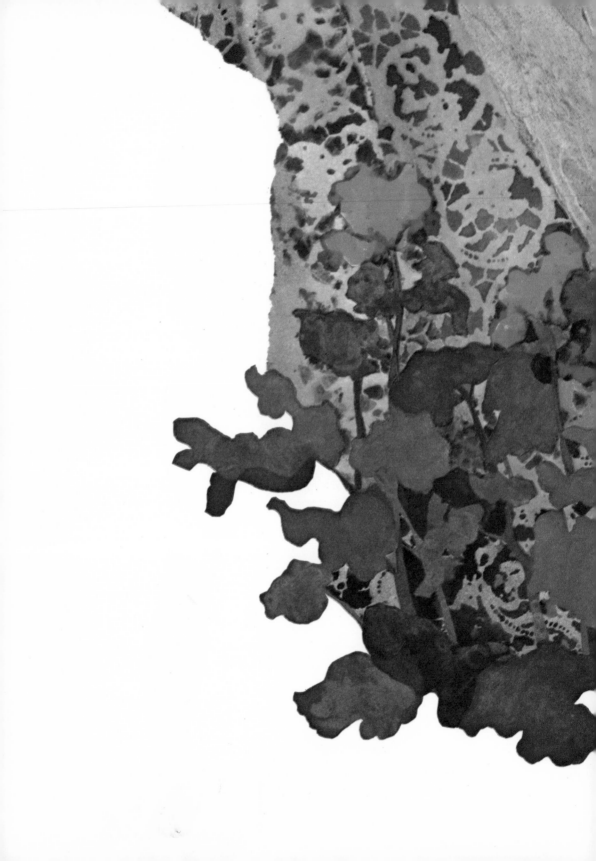

I have a bad dream in the night. I dream that my ears are sucking in every sound in the world, so many sounds I cannot breathe. I am choking with the sounds that are pulled into me and I have to keep coughing the sounds away as they come in or I will smother.

"Here's some stuff for your cold," says my sister.

When I am awake again, I cannot tell if it is morning. I hear noises but they are not the morning noises. My sister has her quiet voice, and I do not hear the little hard sounds of her heels making holes in the morning.

She is wearing slippers. She tells my mother she is not going to go to study today.

There is no hurry about today. I reach for my balloon. The string lies on the chair, and I find the balloon on the floor, small and soft and limp. It does not float. It lies in my hand, tired and sad.

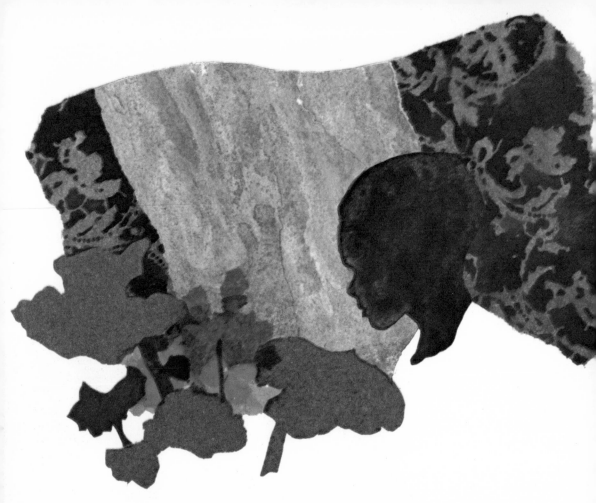

I lie there and listen to the sound of slippers on the kitchen floor.

I tap my good luck song against the wall over and over, but I hear the rain and know I will not go to the park today.

Tomorrow it will be a nice day. Tomorrow my sister will feel better, and I will go to the park and find Abram. He will make my balloon as good as new.

Now I walk over to the window and lean my head against it.

The rain taps its song to me against the glass, and I tap back.

FLORENCE PARRY HEIDE is the author of the recently published *My Castle* and is represented on the Parents' Magazine Press list by *Giants Are Very Brave People*. Besides her many other children's books, she also writes song lyrics in collaboration with composer Sylvia Van Clief, and together they have published several songs and song books.

Mrs. Heide grew up in Pittsburgh where her mother, Florence Fisher Parry, wrote a column for the *Pittsburgh Press*. She is a graduate of the University of California and now lives in Kenosha, Wisconsin with her husband, attorney Donald Heide, and their three sons and two daughters.

KENNETH LONGTEMPS has been illustrating books for children ever since his discharge from the U.S. Air Force in 1955 and has been awarded seven certificates of merit by the Society of Illustrators.

Born in Saranac Lake, New York, Mr. Longtemps received his Bachelor of Fine Arts degree from the Rhode Island School of Design. He now lives with his wife in Brooklyn, New York. His other picture books include *The Day it Snowed in Summer, Danny Dougal,* and *The Little One.*

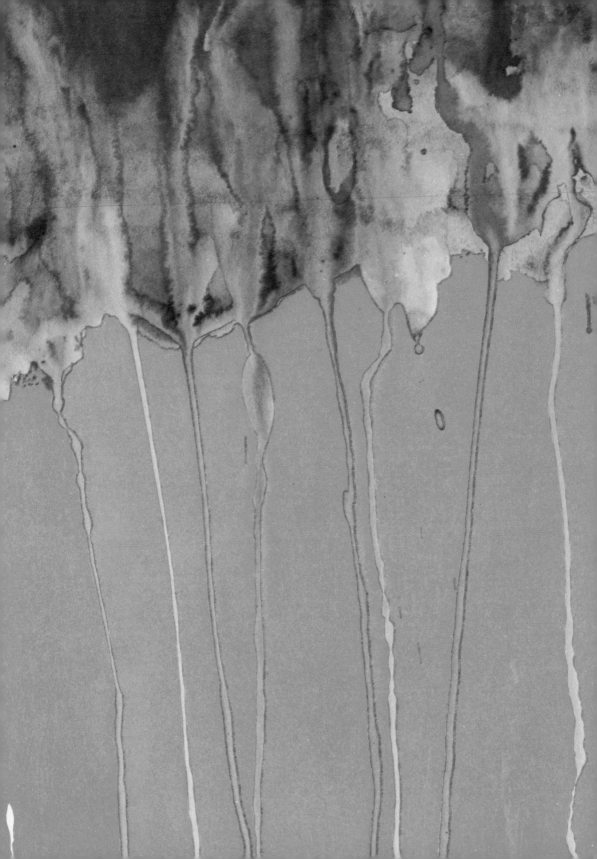

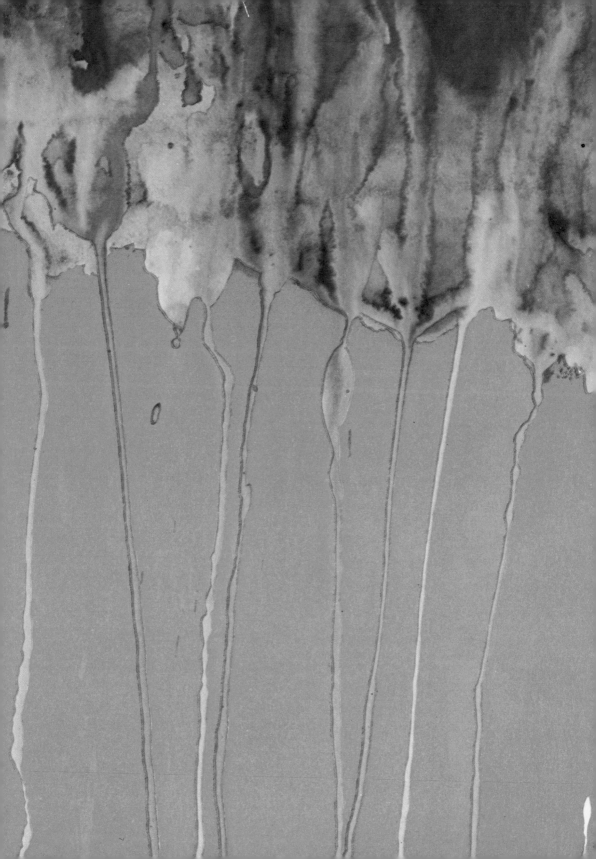